D0914816

ELECTRIC ZOMBIE

PLEASED TO EAT YOU

Calico
An Imprint of Magic Wagon
abdobooks.com

by Johanna Gohmann   illustrated by Aleksandar Zolotić

FOR PORTER AND SAVANNA. I DEAD-ICATE THIS TO YOU. —JG

TO MY DEAR WIFE - WITHOUT YOU, EVEN SETTING UP DAILY SCHEDULE WOULD TURN INTO A HORROR! —AZ

abdobooks.com

Published by Magic Wagon, a division of ABDO, PO Box 398166, Minneapolis, Minnesota 55439. Copyright © 2019 by Abdo Consulting Group, Inc. International copyrights reserved in all countries. No part of this book may be reproduced in any form without written permission from the publisher. Calico™ is a trademark and logo of Magic Wagon.

Printed in the United States of America, North Mankato, Minnesota.
092018
012019

THIS BOOK CONTAINS
RECYCLED MATERIALS

Written by Johanna Gohmann
Illustrated by Aleksandar Zolotić
Edited by Bridget O'Brien
Art Directed by Christina Doffing

Library of Congress Control Number: 2018947812

Publisher's Cataloging-in-Publication Data

Names: Gohmann, Johanna, author. | Zolotić, Aleksandar, illustrator.
Title: Pleased to eat you / by Johanna Gohmann; illustrated by Aleksandar Zolotić.
Description: Minneapolis, Minnesota : Magic Wagon, 2019. | Series: Electric zombie; book 3
Summary: When Zee starts acting stranger than usual, Fab and Lola follow him one night to a secret rock club for older kids, which makes Fab suspect Zee is getting tired of being in their band.
Identifiers: ISBN 9781532133633 (lib. bdg.) | ISBN 9781532134234 (ebook) | ISBN 9781532134531 (Read-to-me ebook)
Subjects: LCSH: Rock groups--Juvenile fiction. | Nightclubs--Juvenile fiction. | Zombies--Juvenile fiction.
Classification: DDC [FIC]--dc23

TABLE OF CONTENTS

CHAPTER 1: YAWNS + FLOATS.....................4

CHAPTER 2: TACO BREAK........................ 17

CHAPTER 3: IS EVERYTHING OKAY?.............. 29

CHAPTER 4: HARDWARE MONSTERS 40

CHAPTER 5: ZEE'S SONG 51

CHAPTER 6: SECRET ROCK CLUB 62

CHAPTER 7: MONSTER CLASH 76

CHAPTER 8: UNDEAD SURPRISE 87

CHAPTER 9: FAN GIRLS + KISSES................ 95

CHAPTER 10: TOO MUCH ZOMBIE ACTION 102

CHAPTER 1

YAWNS + FLOATS

Fab Starr hangs upside down from a tree, his legs hooked over a branch. His friend Zee dangles beside him.

"Hey." Lola smirks as she walks up the path to Emilio's house. "Are we working some gymnastics into the band's next show or something?"

"We're just messing around. We got bored waiting for Emilio."

Lola plops onto a step of Emilio's porch. "You look like a couple of bats in your matching sunglasses."

"Two extremely cool bats, you mean." Fab grins. Just as he says this, his sunglasses come loose from his face and fall to the grass.

"Uh, Fab." Lola squints at him. "Might want to come down now. All the blood is rushing to your head."

Fab swings himself down to the ground, and carefully plucks up his prescription sunglasses. They were a gift from Zee, and mean a lot to him.

Of course, it also means a lot to him that he can see without having to wear his dorky bifocals . . .

"Ha!" Lola suddenly laughs.

"What's so funny?" Fab asks.

"Your hair. How much of your mom's hair goop are you using to get such gravity-defying style?"

"As much as it takes." Fab flops down next to Lola, who wears her leaf-green hair in loose waves.

Zee continues to dangle from the tree. As always, he wears a black hoodie and red leather gloves. His

dark sunglasses appear perfectly balanced on his nose.

"Aren't you getting dizzy, Zee?" Lola calls over.

Fab can't help but notice that Zee's face is still the same ghostly shade of pale it always is. *He doesn't seem to be having a problem with blood rushing to his head . . .* Fab thinks.

The thought makes his stomach roll into knots. It always does when he's reminded of what he knows about Zee.

Zee very slowly lowers himself to the ground, moving at such a creeping pace he resembles a sloth at the zoo. Fab raises his eyebrows at Lola, but she's busy checking texts.

"Where the heck is Emilio? He said to be here at 4:30."

"On his way. Said he needed one last thing from the hardware store before he can unveil his latest invention," Fab says.

"And what is this new invention exactly? I'm scared to ask," Lola says.

Fab shrugs. "Something to do with a guitar."

"A guitar? What's it do? Shoot lightning bolts? Spit hot dogs to the crowd?"

"Who knows. I mean, it's cool he invented something for the band, but I don't think Electric Zombie needs a lot of special effects, you know? I think we're pretty awesome as is."

"Yes. We already awesome. It true," Zee says in his thick accent. He has finally lurched his way to the porch, and lowers himself onto a step.

"There he is! The mad scientist himself!" Lola says.

They watch as Emilio zips up the path on his skateboard.

"So what do you have for us? The world's first nuclear guitar?" Fab teases.

"Alas, the store didn't have what I needed," Emilio says. "So I'll have to show you the guitar another time. But listen, I have awesome news! Guess!"

"Someone invented a hat that can actually contain your hair?" Lola quips.

"Shush." Emilio reaches up to adjust his ball cap. It is jammed over the top of his curly hair. "No, listen to this."

The friends watch Emilio expectantly.

"I was in Howard's Hardware, right? And the owner's daughter comes up to me—"

"Heather Howard? You mean the sophomore?" Lola asks.

"Right! Heather comes up to me, and says she's a huge fan of Electric Zombie. She saw us play Septemberfest."

"Cool," Fab says.

"It gets better! She was glad I came in, because she wanted to see if the band would play on the Howard Hardware float in this year's Halloween parade!"

"What? No way!" Fab jumps off the couch in excitement.

"That's awesome!" Lola shouts.

"Right? The only catch is that Mr. Howard wants us to decorate the float for him," Emilio says.

"We can do that! No problem!" Lola says.

"He wants us to use stuff from the store, and for the float to have some sort of hardware theme."

"A hardware Halloween? Weird, but okay!" Lola nods.

"Practically the whole town comes to the Halloween parade!" Fab says.

"I know! Plus, I think the prize for best float is like, season passes to Whirly Willy's Water Park!" Emilio says.

"Nice!" Fab smiles. He notices Zee hasn't said much about the news. He glances at his friend, and is surprised to see Zee is in the midst of a giant yawn. Fab grimaces at the sight of Zee's oddly yellow teeth.

"Hey . . . aren't you excited, buddy?" Fab asks.

Zee jerks his head up as though his mind has been elsewhere. "Uh. Sure. I have much excitement."

"I know you've never been to the parade here," Lola says. "So, it might sound lame. But trust us, it's fun!"

"It's a blast!" Emilio pops a wheelie on his skateboard.

"Emilio, that isn't the weird skateboard you invented that shoots paintballs, is it?" Fab asks, eyeing the board warily.

"Yeah. But I took all the paintballs out. It's empty, see?" He pops another wheelie, and a red paintball immediately fires out the back, exploding all over the tree in his front yard.

The friends watch silently as red paint oozes down the bark.

"Dude," Fab says. "Your mom is going to kill you."

"Maybe you can tell her it's a redwood?" Lola snickers.

CHAPTER 2

TACO BREAK

"Alright, guys, I think we've earned a break," Fab says.

It's a sunny Saturday, and the band is practicing in Fab's garage. An autumn chill hangs in the air, but everyone is sweaty from exertion.

"Finally! My fingers are starting to feel numb." Emilio slumps away from his keyboard.

Lola unstraps her guitar and collapses on the dusty couch in the corner. Zee leans against the wall and lets his drumsticks clatter to the floor.

"Man, I'm tired too. Anyone for a taco break?"

"Now you're talking!" Emilio says.

"You in, Zee? I know tacos aren't your favorite," Fab says.

Zee shrugs. "A break of the tacos is fine."

"Do they even have tacos in Iceland?" Emilio asks.

Fab watches Zee's face carefully as he answers. "In Iceland? Uh, yes. We have taco. But our toppings are . . . different," Zee mumbles.

I'll bet they are, Fab thinks. He long ago stopped believing Zee and his family had moved to town from Iceland. He isn't sure what strange place they're really from. But he's pretty sure it isn't a Nordic island in the North Atlantic.

"Well, let's go! I'm starving!" Emilio grabs his jacket and heads out into the afternoon light.

"You coming, Lo?" Fab calls to Lola. She rolls off of the couch with a groan.

The friends make their way toward the park and their favorite taco truck—Rocko's Tacos. They kick at the orange and crimson leaves piled along the sidewalk. Realizing that Zee has fallen behind, Fab stops in his tracks.

"Let's wait up," he says.

They watch as Zee lurches his way toward them in his incredibly slow and awkward way.

"I will never understand how someone who moves like a snail can play the drums like he's been set on fire." Emilio shakes his head.

Fab glances at Lola, but she pretends to play with her hair. Fab still hasn't been able to convince her of his suspicions about Zee.

"Is it just me, or does he seem even slower lately?" Emilio says.

Fab doesn't say anything, though he was thinking the same thing. He noticed it the other day when he and Zee were climbing the tree. Zee has always been slow, but lately, it's like he's in super slo-mo mode.

Emilio gives a frustrated sigh. "C'mon, Zee!" he shouts. "I'd like to get my tacos before I'm ninety!"

Zee suddenly freezes in place. Even from this distance, Fab can see his expression slide into a frown. It's hard to read Zee's eyes behind his ever-present sunglasses, but he's pretty sure he looks angry.

"Not cool, Emilio," Fab hisses.

"Yeah, don't be a jerk," Lola whispers.

Zee slides his gloved hands into his hoodie pockets. "You know what?" he calls. "I too slow for you? Go without me." He turns and begins to lurch back toward his house.

"Nice one, Emilio," Lola mutters.

"What's the big deal?" Emilio says. "I just asked him if he could maybe walk at a normal human speed!"

Well, that's hard to do when you aren't even human! Fab wants to shout. But he holds his tongue.

"Emilio, he clearly was moving as quickly as he could. You don't think he'd move faster if he wanted to?" Lola says.

"What, you still think he has some muscle disorder or something?" Emilio asks.

"Well I don't know . . . I don't know what is up with Zee, really."

Lola appears to stumble over her words. Fab notices she's careful not to meet his eyes. "None of us do. Who knows . . . maybe he just didn't want to hang out. Maybe he's sick of us."

"What? Why would he be sick of us?" Fab asks.

Lola shrugs. "Maybe he's tired of being this cool fifteen year old hanging out with thirteen year olds. Did you see him when we told him about the parade? He yawned! Maybe he's bored with the band."

"No way! Zee loves Electric Zombie!" Fab says.

Though even as he says it, he gets a horrible sinking feeling in his stomach.

What if Lola is right, and Zee is sick of them? Or even worse—bored with the band?

"That's dumb." Fab shakes his head. "Zee was just annoyed by Emilio being a jerk."

"Man, now I feel bad. I didn't mean to hurt his feelings," Emilio says. "Should I go apologize? Pretty sure I can catch him."

Fab gazes after Zee. Emilio could definitely catch him, as Zee has barely made it to the corner.

"No. I don't think so. Let him cool off," Lola says. "Anyway, Fab lives directly across the street. He can go by Zee's later and check on him."

Fab says nothing, but gives Lola a look. She knows there is no way Fab is ever going back to Zee's super creepy house.

"Let's get those tacos!" Lola begins to tug them toward the park. "Zee is fine. We're all just hungry and tired."

Fab glances at Zee's retreating figure. He hopes Zee's feelings weren't too hurt. One thing is for sure—he has never had such a confusing friendship in his life. But then, he's never been friends with a zombie.

CHAPTER 3
IS EVERYTHING OKAY?

"So, you didn't get a chance to talk to him last night?" Lola asks.

She and Fab are walking home from school. Emilio had an engineering club meeting, so Fab cancelled practice for the day.

"No, I didn't see him. I thought about sneaking to the high school to find him but didn't have time."

"Why don't you just go knock on his door when you get home? See if he wants to hang out?" Lola suggests.

"Nope." Fab shakes his head. "I am never returning to that house of horrors."

Lola rolls her eyes. "His house was dark and his parents are odd! That's all! You have the most overactive imagination of anyone I have ever met, Fabian Starr."

"And you can't seem to see things right in front of your face, Lola Lega!"

"Oh yeah? Well, I can see our friend Zee. Look, there he is, just down the block."

Fab squints. Sure enough, there's Zee's unmistakable hoodie and trademark lurch. Fab watches as two girls walk past Zee and smile.

"Electric Zombie rules!" one shouts.

Fab has been noticing a lot more of that. Both girls and boys seem to pay a lot of attention to Zee. Fab had even noticed a couple of little kids at school had started wearing red leather gloves.

Zee raises his hand at the girls in a casual, slo-mo wave.

"You know, it's kind of funny," Fab says. "Zee's style is so strange, and he moves so awkwardly. But somehow he still seems . . ."

"Incredibly cool?"

"Yeah," Fab says.

"Well, I mean, aren't the coolest people usually the ones who just don't care what other people think? Most of us are too nervous to be different or weird. But Zee doesn't seem to care."

Fab nods. It's true that some of his favorite rock stars wear weird clothes and dance in weird ways. And their weirdness just makes people love them even more.

"Why don't you run and catch him?" Lola says. "See if he's still mad?"

"Good idea. Alright, I'll catch you tomorrow, Lo."

Fab sprints down the street toward Zee. "Hey buddy. How's it going?" he asks, slightly out of breath.

Zee glances over but keeps walking. "Hey," he mumbles.

"So . . . um . . . Emilio wanted me to apologize for yesterday. He was just joking around," Fab says, fidgeting with the straps on his backpack.

"It fine," Zee mutters.

The friends walk in awkward silence for a moment.

"Is everything okay, Zee?" Fab suddenly blurts out.

Zee stops and looks at Fab stonily. "What you mean? Why things not be okay?"

Something about Zee's tone of voice sends a slight chill down

Fab's spine. He's never quite seen this expression on his friend's face before.

"No, I just mean . . . you seem kind of t-tired or something lately," Fab stammers uneasily. He's never come this close to acknowledging that Zee is different. "I was just wondering if everything is . . . okay?"

Zee stares at him from behind his dark glasses, for several painfully long seconds.

"I fine," he says, then starts walking again.

"Good! Cool!" Fab says. "So, um . . . what are you up to?" His mind races as he tries to think of a way to lighten the conversation. "Do you want to hang out since there's no practice?"

"Hang out?"

"Yeah. Maybe play some video games?" Fab rambles. "My mom just got me the new *Raven Racer*, which is awesome. I also have *Dead Dread—*"

As soon as the words leave Fab's mouth, he can't believe he's said them. *Dead Dread* is a game about zombies! Fab freezes in place, as does Zee.

Zee slowly turns to look at him, and again, Fab feels a chill race down his back. He watches Zee's lips curl slightly, as he slowly raises a gloved hand . . .

But Zee just rakes his hand through his dark hair.

"No thanks," he says. "That game is for kids."

Zee turns and lurches up the walkway to his house. He slowly climbs the steps, then lets his front door slam shut behind him.

Fab stares after him for a moment. The thick woods behind Zee's house are suddenly shaken by the wind. The trees seem to have almost changed color overnight, and the leaves are now a dark, rust red.

The color of blood, Fab thinks.

CHAPTER 4

HARDWARE MONSTERS

Lola stands in her driveway holding a papier-mâché eyeball. The sun sinks behind the trees, and she's squinting into the darkness. "Maybe put this on the shovel monster?"

The parade is only days away, and Fab, Lola, and Emilio are nervously trying to build something for the Howard Hardware float.

A large, wheeled platform sits parked in Lola's driveway. Various hardware tools and crafting supplies lie in heaps at her feet.

Lola hands the eye up to Emilio, who is standing atop the platform.

"Like this?" Emilio attaches the eye to a monster made of wire and fabric. The monster clutches a large shovel.

"A shovel monster? Really?" Fab says.

Lola shrugs. "I asked Mr. Howard to give me an axe or a chain saw, but he said they were too dangerous."

"Great." Fab rolls his eyes. He surveys the hardware store items. Lola's idea is build monsters holding tools around the sides of the float, then the band will play in the middle. Along with the shovel, they have a rake and a toilet plunger.

"And what exactly are you planning to do with that?" Fab eyes the plunger. "Plunger monster? Truly terrifying . . ."

"Are you here to help or complain, Fab?" Lola says. "I'm doing the best I can with what we have."

"Sorry," Fab mumbles, fiddling with a glue gun.

"Can you throw that up to me, buddy?" Emilio asks.

"It's out of glue," Fab grumbles.

"There are glue sticks on my kitchen table. Will you grab some, Emilio?" Lola says.

"Sure. Be right back." Emilio trots up the steps into Lola's house. As soon as he's gone, Lola turns to Fab with a frown.

"What is up with you tonight? This is supposed to be fun, remember?"

Fab says nothing, then heaves a sigh. "I'm sorry. I'm still worried about Zee. I mean, he didn't even show up tonight."

Lola looks at Fab thoughtfully. "It is weird he didn't come to help."

"He didn't even bother to text!" Fab says.

"Are you still worried he thinks we're too babyish or something?" Lola asks.

Fab remembers Zee saying his video game was "for kids." He blushes just thinking about it.

"A little," Fab says. "I mean, that's part of it. But I think something else is going on."

"Relax, Fab. I'm sure there's a simple explanation," Lola says.

"You always think there's a simple explanation!" Fab sighs.

"Because there usually is!"

"Lola," Fab says, his voice dropping to a whisper. "I saw something."

Lola looks at Fab, a strange look on her face. "What do you mean?"

"Well . . . ," Fab says. "The other night after that really late practice, I was in my room, and I glanced out my window toward Zee's."

"And?" Lola asks.

"I saw him leave around midnight, and go into the woods behind his house."

"The woods?"

"Yes," Fab says. "And then I saw him do it again last night."

"So?" Lola shrugs. "Maybe he was just helping his dad collect specimens or something."

Zee's dad is a scientist. Or at least, that's what Zee claims. Zee has told

them before that he sometimes helps his dad with "experiments." But Fab doesn't buy it.

"When I got up for school the next day, I saw Zee returning from the woods. At 6 a.m.! What in the world was he doing in the woods all night?"

"Camping?" Lola suggests.

"Does Zee strike you as the camping type?" Fab hisses.

"Just spit it out! What do you think is going on?" Lola crosses her arms.

She's doing her "tough girl" pose, but Fab can tell by her expression she's a bit frightened by what he might say.

"I think," Fab whispers. "Zee might be going into the woods to . . ."

Lola stares at him.

"To feed . . ." Fab starts to say, but is cut off by Emilio clattering out of Lola's front door.

"Got them!" Emilio shouts.

Fab immediately stops talking. He doesn't like to discuss his Zee theories in front of Emilio. It's bad enough having Lola think he's bonkers. He doesn't need Emilio thinking it too.

Lola quickly leans down and whispers into Fab's ear. "After the next practice, we're following Zee into the woods. Simple as that."

"Whaaa—?" Fab starts to say, but Lola is already climbing up on the float to help Emilio.

Follow him? Are you out of your MIND?! Fab wants to shout. *No way!*

Fab's heart pounds. He stares at the shovel monster, and it stares back. It's giant, ghoulish eye glints under the streetlight.

CHAPTER 5
ZEE'S SONG

Fab pulls his guitar strap off his neck and runs a hand through his hair. "Everyone ready for Sunday?"

The band is finishing up their final practice before the parade. The atmosphere in Fab's garage is usually lighthearted and fun.

But tonight feels oddly tense, and everyone seems on edge. Zee hasn't said a single word to anyone the entire night.

"Totally." Lola nods, though she sounds uneasy. "I mean, once the float's finished tomorrow, of course."

"I can't believe we're going to perform in front of the whole town," Emilio says. "No way am I going to be able to sleep the next two nights. Guess I better get home so I can start tossing and turning . . ."

He begins to pack up his things.

"Wait!" Zee shouts. "I have something I want share. With band."

Fab jerks his head toward Lola, and she looks at Fab with wide eyes. Fab's mind starts racing. *Is Zee about to tell the band the truth?*

"Sure," Fab tries to sound calm. "What's up?"

"I have write new song," Zee says quietly. "I would like to share."

Lola breathes a sigh of relief. "A new song?" She smiles. "Cool! Let's hear it!"

Fab watches as Zee lurches out from behind his drum kit. Fab is the only one who ever shares new songs.

Zee has certainly helped Fab a lot with songwriting—offering tips on beat and chord changes. But Fab didn't realize he wrote his own stuff.

"Lay it on us, Zee!" Emilio flops onto the couch.

"May I?" Zee holds out a gloved hand to Fab's guitar.

Fab looks at his friend, and not for the first time, wishes he could read what is going on behind his sunglasses. He silently hands over his instrument, then joins Emilio and Lola on the couch.

Zee places a crumpled piece of paper on the floor and glances down at it. He strums an opening chord, then drops his head back in a dramatic pose.

Fab expects him to launch into a lightning fast beat, similar to what he does on the drums. But instead, he begins a slow, haunting melody. It somehow sounds mournful and weirdly sweet at the same time.

Zee's singing voice, Fab is shocked to discover, is deep and soulful. It's much louder than his speaking voice, and there's no trace of his accent.

Out of the corner of his eye, Fab can see Emilio and Lola exchanging looks of surprise.

Zee sings: "The sun trips and falls

"The moon begins its eager rise

"While I sit alone in shadows

"And quietly count out sighs

"I try to walk among the light

"To smile and wave and do it all right . . .

"But . . .

"I am DEAD

"So dedicaaaaated . . .

"I am DEAD

"So dedicaaaated . . .

"To finding

"What is true

"What is real

"What will finally make me feel

"Alive."

Zee strums the final note, then looks at them. The room is so quiet Fab can hear the faint hum of an overhead light bulb.

"Zee!" Emilio finally exclaims. "That was awesome!"

"Dude." Lola looks at Emilio in amusement. "Are you crying?"

"No!" Emilio rubs his eyes. "But I mean . . . c'mon, it was super sad! It just really captures, you know . . ."

Fab gulps, waiting to hear what Emilio will say next. " . . . loneliness! And trying to fit in, and all that junk."

"No, I agree." Lola nods. "It's a really beautiful song, Zee."

"And Fab?" Zee says softly. "What you think?"

Fab's mind is racing. He thought the song was amazing, but he can't get past the lyrics! *I am dead?!?*

"It's great," he manages to croak.

Zee cocks his head and seems to watch Fab for a minute.

"Alright," he says. "I go now." And with that, he turns and lurches out into the night, leaving the three friends to stare after him.

"Man. Just when I think that dude can't surprise me anymore," Emilio says. "Alright, I seriously gotta go. And I wasn't crying, okay? I think there's a gnat problem in here or something."

Emilio quickly gathers up his things and zips away on his skateboard.

Fab walks over and plucks up the crumpled lyrics Zee left on the floor. He peers at the scribbly handwriting: *DEADICATED. A song by Zee.*

He waves the paper at Lola. "Still up for following our friend into the woods tonight?" he asks.

CHAPTER 6

SECRET ROCK CLUB

Fab and Lola sit in Fab's dark kitchen. It's almost midnight, but they are wide awake, and peering across the street at Zee's house.

"You're sure your mom's asleep?" Lola whispers.

"Yeah. She has an early morning conference. What did you tell your dad?" Fab whispers back.

"I said I was staying at Josie's," Lola says. "Josie will cover for me."

"Cool. How is Josie, by the way? Is she coming to the parade?" Fab asks, his voice raising a bit. He always struggles to sound casual when asking about Josie—Lola's very cool, very pretty older cousin.

"Oh, she wouldn't miss it. She's like, our biggest fan," Lola says.

"Cool," Fab mumbles, trying to conceal his rush of excitement. *Our biggest fan . . .*

"Wait!" Lola hisses. "There he is!"

Across the street, Zee slowly walks out of his house. He pauses for a moment on the sidewalk.

For one sick moment, Fab feels certain he sees them! Then he turns, and makes his way into the woods.

Fab and Lola quietly creep out the front door to follow him. It's a moonless night, and the woods look like an endless black void.

"You really think this is necessary?" Lola whispers.

"What?!?" Fab stares at her. "Following him was *your* idea!"

"I know but . . . now I'm not really sure why we're doing it."

Fab looks at her in disbelief.

"Lola, what more do you need? He sang a song tonight about being dead! He may as well have worn a name tag that said, 'Hello! I am a zombie!'"

"Or it was just a song about fitting in!" Lola sputters. "It wouldn't be so crazy for the new kid in town to write a song about loneliness!"

Fab shakes his head. "I need to know what's going on, Lola."

"Just because things get weird with a friend, you can't decide it's because they're a monster," Lola says. "If you and I fight, will you become convinced I'm secretly a witch?"

"Right now I'm convinced you're a big chicken!" Fab hisses.

"Fine!" Lola throws up her hands. "Let's go!"

They slowly make their way into the woods. Fab climbs over a fallen branch, and his jacket catches on some thorns. He flips on his phone light to guide them.

"Are we sure that's him?" Lola whispers.

Fab peers through the clusters of trees at the distant figure ahead. "Well, unless that's a slow-motion grizzly bear wearing a hoodie, yeah, I'm sure."

They follow Zee for several minutes. Then he seems to suddenly step into a clearing, and disappear down a hill.

Fab freezes. "Do you hear that?"

Lola looks at him. "Music?" she mouths silently.

Fab tilts his head. He hears the unmistakable speed and roar of a punk rock song. He gestures for Lola to follow him, and they slowly make their way to the spot where Zee left the woods.

When they get to the clearing, Fab can hardly believe his eyes.

At the bottom of the hill is a swarm of people. They're dancing around in the darkness in front of an abandoned warehouse. Two people stand on a rickety wooden platform, thrashing away at guitars.

"Is it some kind of secret rock club?" Lola whispers.

Fab just stares. It's hard for him to tell from this distance, but everyone seems much older. Maybe even older than Zee.

They also look really . . . rough. Their clothes seem ripped and tattered, and they dance in a wild, angry way.

"What high school are they from?" Lola asks, her eyes wide.

Fab notices one guy in particular. Something about him makes Fab's scalp prickle in fear. He's incredibly tall, with a scraggly yellow Mohawk.

Fab watches as he whips his head around to the music, then walks over to what looks like a food truck.

Painted on the side of the truck is a large purple brain. Above the brain it reads: *Brainy Burgers—Food for hungry young minds!*

The guy reaches up to take something from the truck. Then he ravenously eats it, like an animal tossed a piece of raw meat.

The ferocious-sounding punk song ends, and the crowd whoops. Fab and Lola watch as a new group of people climb onto the platform.

"Is that Zee?" Lola elbows Fab, and points to a boy in a hoodie holding two drumsticks. Even in all the chaos, Fab feels a surge of anger. *Is Zee playing with another band?!?*

He wishes they could move closer, but doing so would mean stepping out of the woods and exposing themselves. Something they most certainly do not want to do!

The crowd quiets as the group on stage gets ready to play. Suddenly, from Fab's jeans comes the blast of his cell phone.

Lola turns, a panicked look on her face. Fab fumbles to pull his phone out of his pocket. Down below, he's certain a few heads turn toward the ringing . . . including a head with a scraggly yellow Mohawk.

Fab quickly pulls Lola back into the woods, out of sight. He glances at the phone.

Incoming call from: Mom.

Fab pulls Lola back toward home. With a deep breath, he hits "accept call." He doesn't even get a word out before his mom begins shouting.

"Fabian Isaac Starr! Where are you? Do you know how worried I was when you weren't in your bed?"

"Sorry Mom! I . . . went for a walk. I was . . . nervous about the parade," Fab stammers out an excuse.

"A walk? At midnight? You better be back in five minutes mister, or expect to be grounded the rest of your life!"

"On my way!" Fab hangs up as he and Lola race through the woods, leaping over fallen tree trunks.

"You still okay sleeping on the couch in the garage?" Fab calls over to her.

"Yes!" Lola calls back breathlessly.

After tonight, I don't see either of us getting much sleep! Fab thinks. In the distance behind them, he can faintly hear the opening strains of another thumping punk song.

CHAPTER 7

MONSTER CLASH

Fab lies in bed, wearily rubbing at his eyes. He hasn't slept a wink.

After sneaking Lola into the garage, he went into the house and listened to his mom lecture him for twenty minutes.

By the time he crawled into bed, he was still wound up. He just stared at the ceiling until dawn.

It's Saturday, but he gets up and sneaks to the garage. He finds a note on the couch: *Will talk later. — Lo*

Fab heads inside and begins doing chores, hoping to appease his mom. He still fears she might ground him from the parade.

He distractedly runs the vacuum while images of brainy burgers float through his head. The night before now feels like a bizarre dream.

At dinner, neither Fab nor his mom speak. Finally, Fab takes a breath and turns to her.

"So, I'm supposed to meet the band tonight to finish the float," he mumbles.

His mom puts down her fork and frowns at him.

"That's fine. You've already committed to Mr. Howard and the parade. And you need to honor that commitment. But going forward, if the band is causing you so much anxiety you need to take midnight strolls, we might need to rethink whether you're old enough to be in a rock band."

Fab nods, then grabs his jacket and races to Lola's house.

He arrives to see Lola in her driveway. She is blearily watching Emilio crawl around the float amid a small pile of electrical cords.

"Hang on! I almost have it working!" Emilio calls down.

Fab leans over to Lola. "Can you believe last night?" he whispers.

Lola runs a hand through her green hair and sighs. "Well, I actually think it all makes sense now."

Fab looks at her in confusion.

"Zee's obviously been sneaking off to that weird club. No wonder he's been acting strangely and moving so slowly. He's exhausted. And those people looked pretty . . . weird. Who knows what he gets up to when he hangs out with them."

"You've got to be kidding!" Fab hisses. "You seriously think that was just some secret rock club, and those were *regular* people? Did you not *see* those people?"

"I saw those people from a distance, in the dark, just like you,"

Lola replies. "And yeah, they looked strange. They were also clearly into punk. Punk rockers aren't known for their conservative style, Fab."

Fab opens his mouth to protest, but Emilio calls to them: "Ready? Here goes!"

Emilio flips a switch. Fab and Lola gaze at the float. The hardware monsters—rake monster, shovel monster, and yes, plunger monster— move their heads up and down.

"Isn't it great?" Emilio grins. "I rigged it up so they're bopping their heads to the beat! When we play, it will look like they're dancing!"

Fab says nothing. He doesn't want to hurt Emilio's feelings, but it kind of looks like the monsters are nodding, not dancing.

"It looks . . ." Lola says hesitantly.

"Why are monsters saying 'yes, yes, yes'?" says a low voice behind them.

Fab jumps, and is shocked to see Zee suddenly standing behind him.

"Sorry. I not mean to scare," Zee says. "I come to see float."

Nice of you to show up! Fab wants to shout. But he says nothing.

"This is it!" Lola gestures. "What do you think?"

"Wait, does it really look like the monsters are saying 'yes, yes, yes'?" Emilio moans.

"Yes," Zee says. "It does."

"Aw man!" Emilio fidgets with the pile of wires again.

Zee walks slowly around the float. "It big. We play in this space here?" He points to the middle.

"Yep! So do you like it?" Lola asks.

"Well." Zee gazes up at the rake. "The monsters . . . they not so scary." Fab can see Lola's face cloud. "We kind of did the best we could, Zee—"

"I will fix," Zee cuts her off. "Tomorrow at parade I bring something for float to make extra scary."

He turns, and gives Fab a small, strange smile. "See you tomorrow, then," he says, then lurches into the shadows.

Fab turns to Lola and can tell she's fuming.

"Nice! Zee doesn't help at all, then just shows up and says it's lame?" She crosses her arms angrily.

"Not cool," Fab agrees.

He really doesn't know what to think of Zee anymore. He's never seen this side of his friend.

Although, Fab thinks. *Probably no one knows better than Zee what monsters should really look like . . .*

"Okay. How about now?" Emilio shouts, flipping another switch. The monsters' heads move from side to side.

"Great," Lola sighs. "Now they're all saying 'no, no, no.'"

CHAPTER 8

UNDEAD SUPRISE

Fab, Lola, and Emilio stand anxiously atop the float, which is parked in a side alley. It's hitched to a truck from Howard Hardware. Electric Zombie's instruments are loaded on top, ready to go.

Heather Howard sits in the truck next to her dad. She peeks at Fab, giving him a nervous thumbs-up.

Fab tries to look calm. The parade is due to start in ten minutes, and as usual, there's no sign of Zee.

"I can't believe I couldn't get the monsters to work," Emilio grumbles.

"Let it go, Emilio," Lola snaps. "The float is fine!"

"I'm sorry Lo, but I feel super lame standing next to a plunger," Emilio sighs. "Man, I hope whatever Zee is bringing is good . . ."

I just hope Zee shows up! Fab thinks. But he doesn't say it, for fear of panicking everyone.

"Well, at least it isn't raining," he says instead. He casts his eyes at the dark, cloudy sky. "Not yet, anyway."

Suddenly, in the alley behind them, they hear a small commotion. They all turn toward the noise.

"What the . . ." Lola whispers.

The shouting grows louder. Out of the shadows emerges Zee, leading a small pack of people. As they move closer, Fab's mouth drops open.

The group are in torn, muddy clothes, and their hair is wild and dirty.

Their mouths are rimmed in a crusty red, and their faces are sickly pale and covered in sores. They're also wearing sunglasses like Zee's.

Fab spies an extremely tall boy with a scraggly, yellow Mohawk, and his mouth goes completely dry.

"Dude!" Emilio laughs. "No way! You brought zombies!"

Zee lurches closer. "Yes." He smiles. "These are friends from . . . uh, rock club I go to."

"Cool!" Emilio says. "Which club? The Black Arrow?"

"Uh . . . no. This club for . . . older kids," Zee says. Fab looks at Lola, and is stunned to see she looks excited!

"My friends . . . they dress up like zombies to help with float. They will dance on float while we play."

"Zee, you're brilliant!" Emilio says. Zee and his friends climb aboard.

"Everyone's makeup is so . . . realistic!" Lola says.

"Glad you like." Zee smiles. "I know you think I not care about float, Lola friend. But see . . . I bring zombies and now float is scary, yes?"

That's for sure! Fab thinks. The yellow Mohawk boy flashes him a ghastly grin.

"He is called Wilder." Zee gestures to the Mohawk boy.

Fab raises his eyebrows. "Wilder?"

"Because he . . . a . . . wild dancer," Zee says. His friends all snicker. "He stand near front and show off his moves."

Just then, the float lurches forward. Fab is still trying to take in what's happening, but there's no time! The parade is starting!

Zee claps a gloved hand on Fab's shoulder and leans in close. He whispers into his ear: "Relax, Fab. It is our favorite time. The time in which we rock."

He gives Fab's shoulder a squeeze, then lurches toward his drum kit.

Fab quickly fumbles to pull on his guitar and step behind the microphone.

In the truck, he can see Heather staring at the zombies. She claps excitedly, and gives Fab another, much more enthusiastic thumbs-up.

CHAPTER 9
FAN GIRLS
+ KISSES

The float pulls onto Main Street and falls in line with the rest of the parade. Zee taps out the beat to Electric Zombie's loudest, fastest song. His zombie friends go wild dancing.

Emilio and Lola exchange looks of amusement, while Fab tries to calm a rising feeling of panic.

The float coasts down the street into a horde of people. Their faces light up as they cruise past.

Despite the confusion and craziness, Fab feels a huge jolt of excitement. The crowd cheers as Zee's friends flail, in a mad swirl of color and thumping drums.

With a deep breath, Fab turns toward the mic, and does what he loves most in the world: strums his guitar and sings. His voice booms out of the speakers, and seems to echo through the streets.

Parade-goers dance and laugh. Little kids sit on shoulders and point at the float with wide eyes.

A group of girls shout Fab's name. They wave posters that say *I Love Electric Zombie!* Fab grins at them, and they shriek with excitement.

Fab spies someone holding up a large, handmade sign painted with a blood-red *Z* inside a black heart. The person lowers the sign to cheer. He immediately recognizes the short purple hair of Josie, Lola's cousin.

"Go Zee!" she shouts.

Josie catches Fab's eye and shoots him a huge smile. Fab grins back, and tries to ignore the flash of jealousy that she's holding a sign for Zee.

They move down the street, then turn into the last leg of the route. The other floats move quietly. But whenever they approach, the crowd lets out a roar of delight.

Zee launches into their next song—another fast number. Again, his friends dance like maniacs. Wilder throws his body around. *He is an amazing dancer*, Fab has to admit.

He moves like he doesn't have real bones. *Maybe he doesn't?* says a small voice in Fab's head. He tries to shake the thought away.

Wilder dances his way over to Lola and throws an arm over her shoulder. Lola smiles, and tosses her green hair, thrashing away at her bass. Fab watches as Wilder's mouth moves toward Lola.

Is he trying to kiss her? Fab thinks in bewilderment.

Wilder leans in. Fab sees a flash of yellow teeth, just as the float bumps

the curb and jumps slightly. Fab watches as Lola pushes Wilder away with a scream.

Wilder leaps off the moving float and runs down a side street! Zee's other friends quickly do the same, leaping and lurching after Wilder.

They disappear into the shadows.

The crowd whoops and cheers, clearly thinking this is all part of the show.

Fab drops his guitar and runs over to Lola. He's surprised when Zee gets to her first.

Zee grabs hold of Lola and shouts over the noise of the crowd. "Lola friend! You okay?!"

"He tried to bite my ear!" Lola says.

Fab watches in fear, as Zee's already pale face seems to go several shades whiter.

CHAPTER 10
TOO MUCH ZOMBIE ACTION

The float slowly rolls to the end of the route, and Zee carefully examines Lola's ear. A look of relief washes over his face.

"You are fine," Zee sighs, patting Lola on the head.

"Great!" Fab shouts angrily. "Now maybe you can explain why that weirdo tried to bite her?"

Zee glances at Fab, then looks away. "He . . . he not trying to bite! He trying to kiss! It just float! It shaky!" As if to prove his point, the float suddenly jerks to a stop.

"I sorry Lola friend!" Zee shouts. "Wilder just . . . wild guy!"

Fab starts to shout back, but all around them the crowd is exploding into cheers. Fab suddenly realizes everyone is staring up at them, and Emilio grabs his arm.

"Fab! Did you not hear the announcement? We won best float!"

Fab looks around in confusion. He sees Heather Howard and her dad standing in the street.

The mayor hands Mr. Howard a small trophy, and gives Heather a colorful packet of tickets. Heather grins at the band, and waves the tickets at them.

"Yes!" Emilio says. "Season passes to Whirly Willies, here we come!"

The rest of the afternoon races by. Fab shakes a very happy Mr. Howard's hand, and poses for selfies with fans.

When people ask Fab where the dancing zombies got their "awesome costumes", he just shrugs and smiles tightly. He gets a hug from Josie, but he can't help but notice she seems to hug Zee a few seconds longer.

That evening, Fab and Zee walk home together in a heavy silence. Dark clouds still loom, and now thunder can be heard rumbling in the distance.

Fab's mind races with the day's events. There's a lot he wants to say, but he has no idea where to begin.

"I owe band apology," Zee says, and Fab looks at him in surprise.

"I not been good bandmate lately. Or good friend." Zee fidgets with his sunglasses. "My life . . . it complicated," he mutters.

Fab is surprised by the sadness in Zee's voice. He watches his friend lurch along beside him, and despite himself, he can feel his anger lifting.

"It's alright," Fab says.

"It is?" Zee says quietly.

"Sure." Fab shrugs. "All the great bands fight sometimes, right?"

"This true." Zee smiles. "Oh . . . before I forget." He hands Fab a card. Fab sees it's Zee's season pass for the water park. "This Whirly Willies . . . it not really Zee's thing."

Fab pictures Zee shooting down a water slide in his hoodie and leather gloves, and can't help but chuckle.

"Yeah," Fab says. "I imagine not."

As they approach their houses, Fab notices a figure standing at the edge of the woods. He squints, and quickly recognizes a scraggly, yellow Mohawk blowing in the breeze.

Zee follows Fab's gaze. "Wilder here. We meeting friends at club."

Fab eyes Wilder's tattered clothes and sunglasses. "Still in his zombie costume, huh?" Fab says, carefully watching Zee's face.

"He . . . no have time to change," Zee mumbles.

"Right." Fab nods slowly.

Wilder beckons for Fab to come closer, and Fab nervously follows Zee over to the woods. "Sorry about yer friend," Wilder growls in a low, gravelly voice.

"Sh-she's fine," Fab stammers.

"You wanna come too?" Wilder jerks his head toward the woods, flashing Fab a yellow-toothed grin.

Fab peers through the trees. He can see the shadowy figures of Zee's friends in the distance. Fab gasps, as his blood seems to turn to ice.

He is certain he sees several pairs of glowing green eyes in the dark. Fab has seen those eyes before.

He feels a hand clamp sharply on his back, and Zee leans down to him, his face like stone.

"You go home now. This crowd too . . . old for you," Zee says.

Fab says nothing, just turns and sprints through the darkness toward his house. He can hear Wilder's dry cackle chasing after him. *Is he following me?!?* Fab's heart pounds in his ears.

Almost home, he stumbles over something in his front yard and lands flat in the grass. He turns and sees two long zombie arms reaching for his face! He lets out a bloodcurdling scream!

"Goodness, Fab!" says a voice. Fab looks up and sees his mom standing over him, shaking her head.

"I guess you like my Halloween decorations, then?" she says.

She leans down and adjusts two rubber zombie arms sticking out of the ground.

"Or have you had enough zombie action for one day?" She smiles.

His hands shaking, Fab looks back toward the woods. But no one is there. He sits up and heaves a heavy sigh.

"Mom," Fab mutters. "You have no idea."